This Book Belongs To

. . . .

This edition first published 1999
by Hodder Children's Books

10 9 8 7 6 5 4 3 2

A Catalogue record for this book is available from the British Library.

ISBN 0 340 71365 8

Printed and bound in Great Britain by
Omnia Books Ltd, Glasgow

Hodder Children's Books
A Division of Hodder Headline Limited
338 Euston Road
London NW1 3BH

Space Dog Meets Space Cat

Vivian French

Illustrated by Sue Heap

a division of Hodder Headline Limited

For E.P

Chapter One

It was the middle of the afternoon, and very quiet.

Big Sun was dozing on a cloud.

Little Sun was swinging on his swing.

"Space Dog!" Little Sun called. "Look how high I can go!"

Space Dog was polishing his doorstep. "Don't go too high, Little Sun," he said. "You might fall off!"

"No I won't," Little Sun said. "I'm a good swinger!"

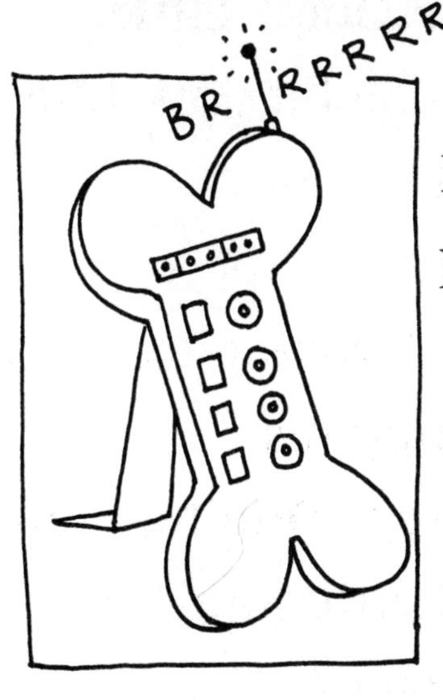

It was the bone phone.

Space Dog hurried inside his kennel.

"EEEK!!
EEEK!!!
EEEEEEK!!!!"

Space Dog held the phone away from his ear.

"Space mouse," he said. "Calm down!"

Far away, Space Mouse took a deep breath.

"Space Dog . . . you've got to DO something about the HOWLING and the MEOWLING! My babies can't sleep! It's just TERRIBLE! EEK! EEK! EEEEK!"

Space dog hung up and shook his head.
"Meowling? Who could that be? I'd better have a little fly around. It never hurts to check things out . . . "

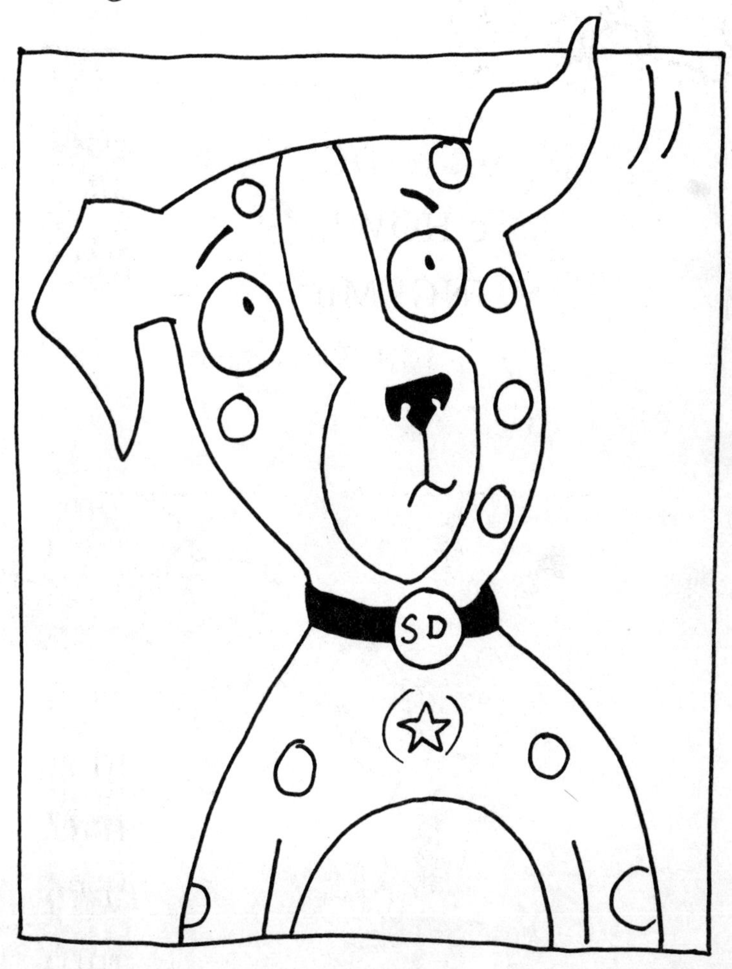

Outside, Little Sun was
swinging higher and
higher.
"Look how high
I'm going! Look,
Space Dog—
OOOOOHH!"
Little Sun
tumbled off
his swing—

down . . .
and down . . .

and down.

ZOOOOOOOMMM!!!
Space Dog zoomed after
Little Sun.

Up above, Big Sun sat up on his cloud and rubbed his eyes.

"Help!" shouted Little Sun as he fell faster and faster. "Help!"

"Woof! I'm coming, Little Sun!" Space Dog did a dive and a double double flip.

THWACKK! Space Dog and Little Sun crashed together and bounced apart –

and Little Sun found himself flying up . . . and up . . . and into Big Sun's arms.

"Little Sun!" said Big Sun. "Don't you EVER do that again!"

Space Dog was dizzy.

He didn't know if he was flying or floating. His head was swimming and he was seeing big red and yellow stars.

They were
whirling and
twirling in
front of his eyes.

"OW!" Space Dog groaned.
"My POOR head … "
And as he held his poor sore head in his paws he drifted away into a maze of burnt-out meteors.

Chapter Two

"WOOF!!!" Space Dog stared round. "Where am I? It's EVER so dark. I think I'd better get out of here – as soon as I can!"

He flew in between two large craggy rocks - but hundreds of little rocks were spinning behind them.
Space Dog braked hard.

"Whoops! Not this way! I'll try the other way."

The other
way was
just as
bad.

Space Dog
couldn't fly
up . . .

. . . and he
couldn't fly
down.

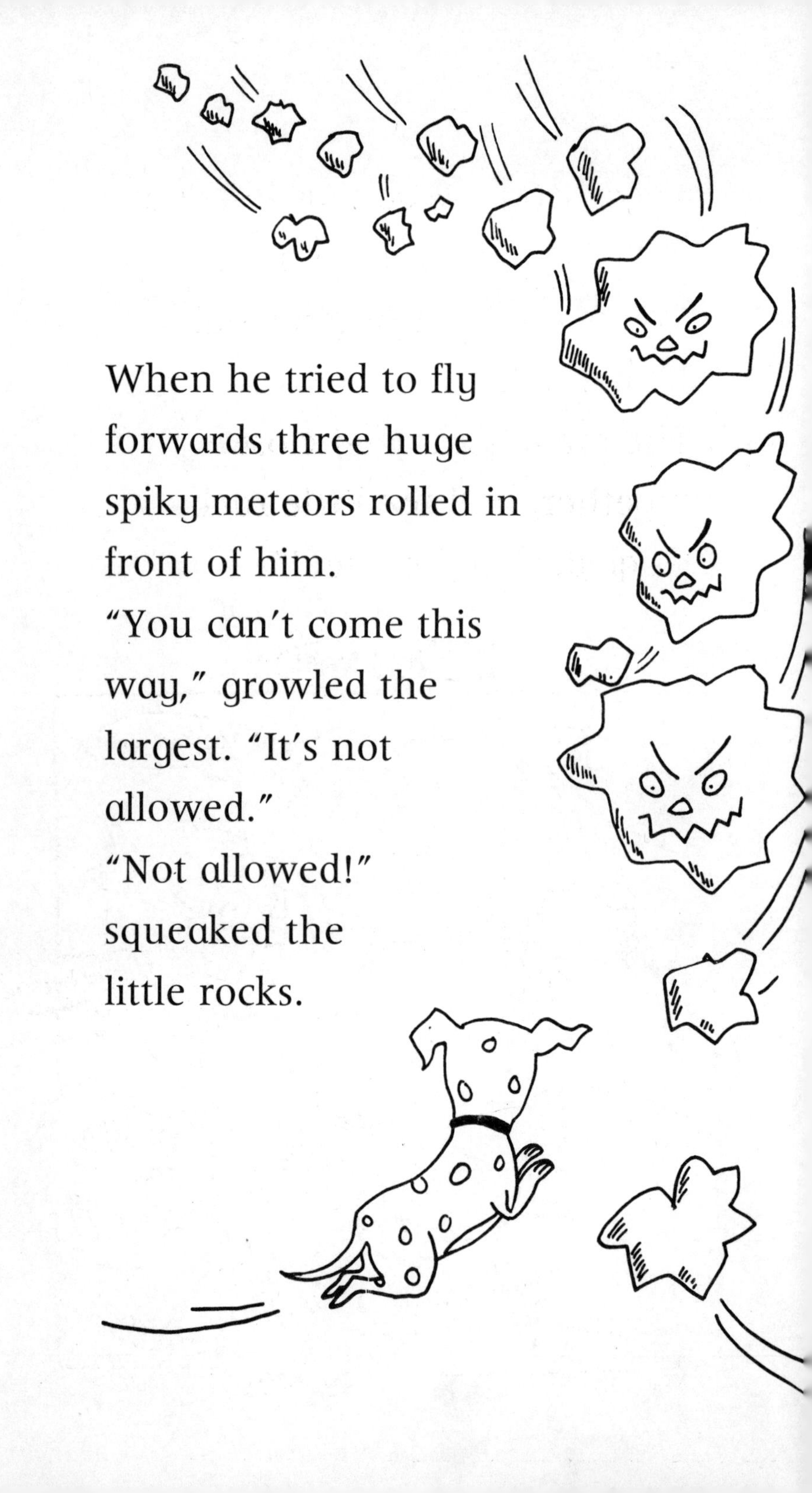

When he tried to fly
forwards three huge
spiky meteors rolled in
front of him.
"You can't come this
way," growled the
largest. "It's not
allowed."
"Not allowed!"
squeaked the
little rocks.

Space Dog's head was hurting
and he wanted to go home.
"Woof! Get out of my way!"
he barked.
The meteors moved closer
together, and the little rocks
giggled. "Tee hee hee!"

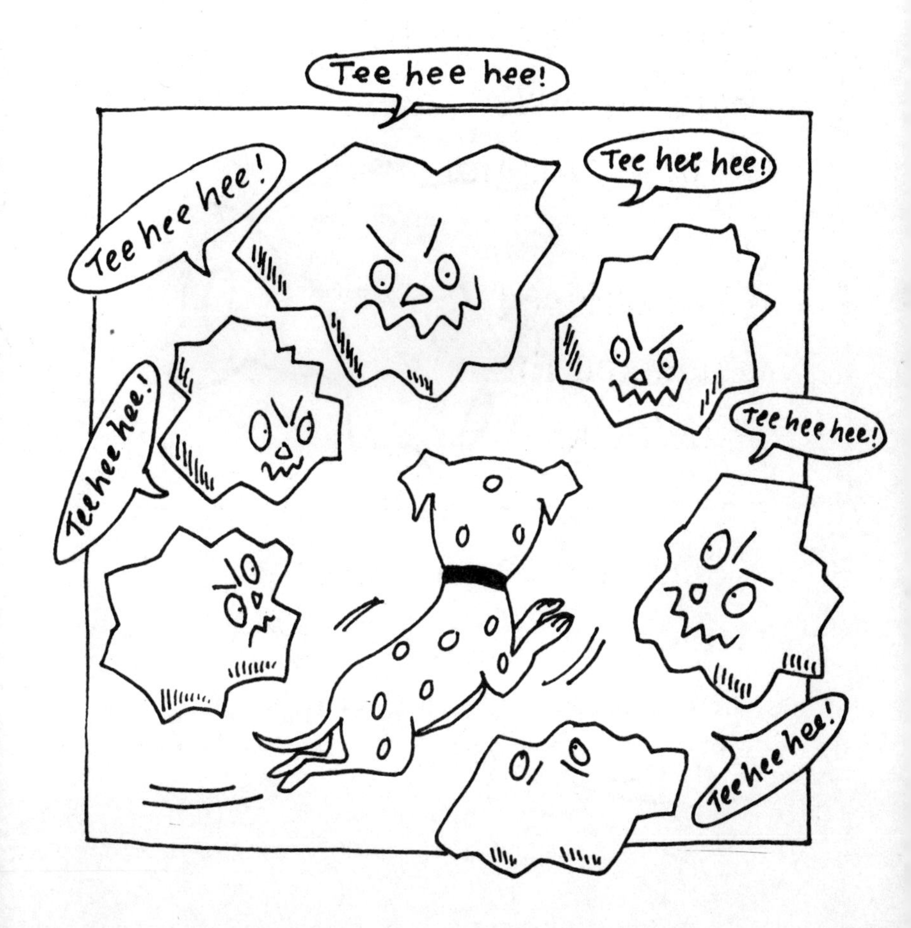

Space Dog spun round and landed on the largest meteor. "OI!" The meteor shook all over in fury. "That's not allowed!"

"Says who?" asked Space Dog, rudely.
The meteor shut its eyes and sulked.

Space Dog stood on the meteor and peered into the grey mist. It was hard to see anything at all.

He sat down. "Woof," he said. "Things aren't looking too good. Whatever shall I—"

Space Dog leapt to his feet. "That must be the noise Space Mouse was hearing! No wonder it kept her babies awake!"

Space Dog scrambled away on to a large rock. Behind him the meteor went on grumbling.

A few minutes later Space Dog stopped for breath.
"PHEW!" he puffed. "It's further than I thought."
He pricked up his ears and listened again.

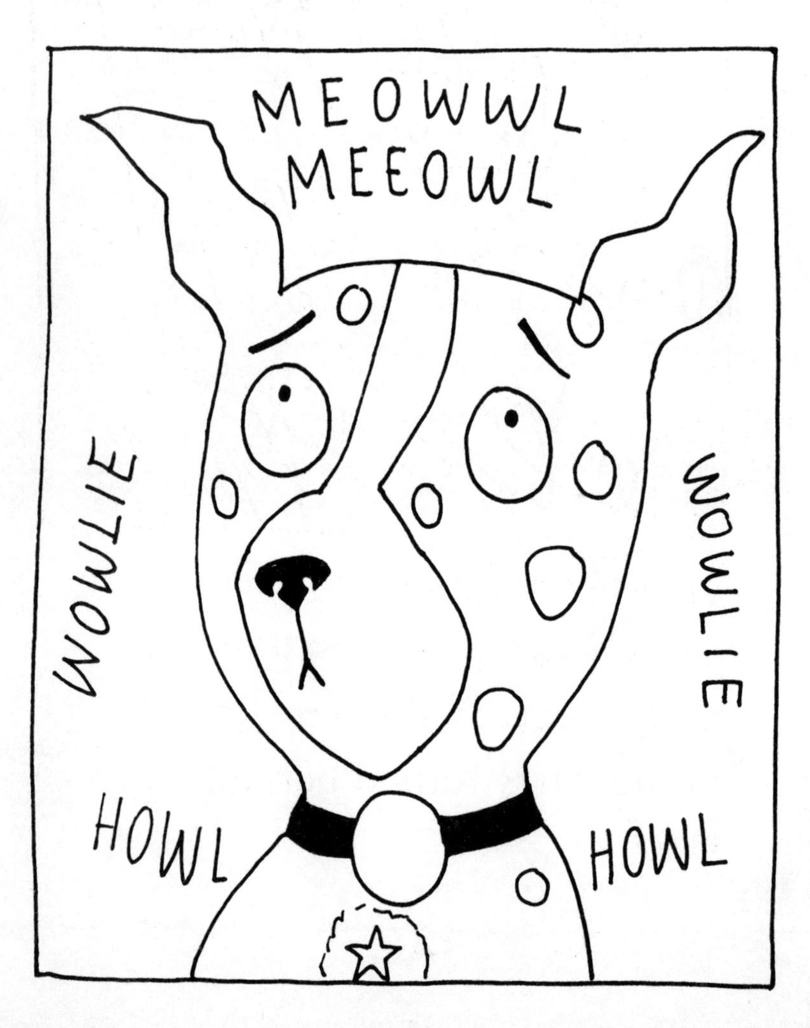

"There it is. Now – if I can just squeeze through here . . . OWWWWW!"

Space Dog found himself slithering and sliding down a steep slope. A shower of little stones rattled behind him.

At once,
hundreds
of Threepies
popped out
to watch.

"WUZZZ! WUZZZ! Space Dog!" they buzzed, and they waggled their antennae.

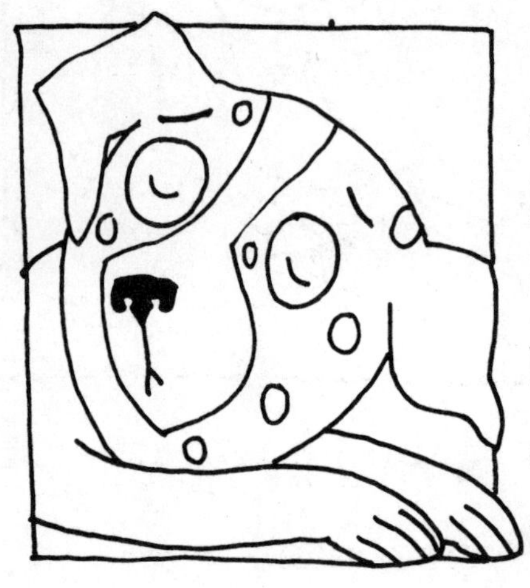

Space Dog lay still with his eyes shut. "This has been a BAD day," he said to himself.

"A VERY bad day."

Something meeowed in Space Dog's ear. He opened his eyes and saw a strange and stripy creature.

Space Dog stared. “Who are you?” he asked.
“Space Cat,” said the creature. “How do you do.”

Chapter Three

Space Dog sat up very carefully. His head was spinning again.

"Space Cat!" he said. "Well I never ... I mean ... pleased to meet you!"

Space Cat
smiled and
began to purr.

Space Dog
rubbed his
nose with a
dusty paw.

"I don't mean to be rude, but this
isn't the sort of place I'd expect
to find someone like you."

Space Cat's whiskers trembled. "But I don't belong here. I had a dear little planet of my very own . . . Planet Purrgo. It was SO cosy . . . just me and a few Threepies."

"So what happened?" asked Space Dog.

Space Cat sighed. "I went out one evening – and when I came back my planet was gone! I've been looking for it ever since . . ."

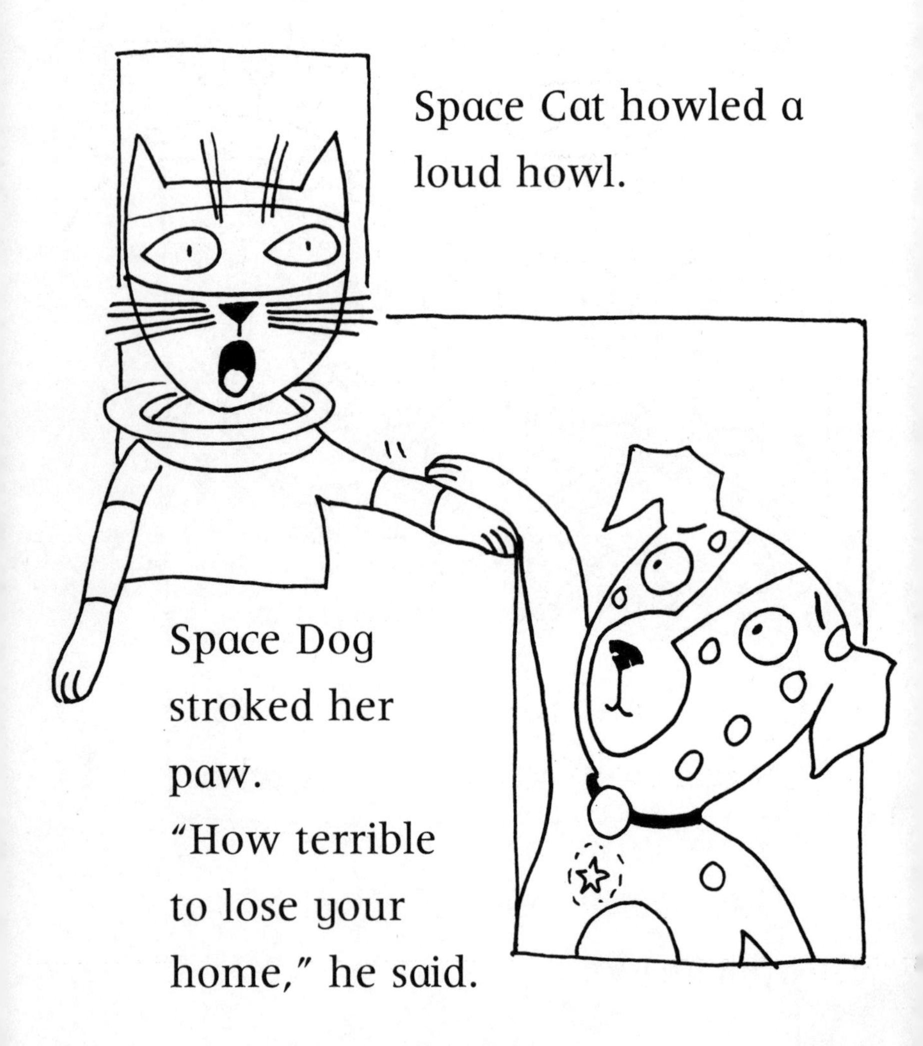

Space Cat howled a loud howl.

Space Dog stroked her paw.
"How terrible to lose your home," he said.

"Pink Arkle told me that Threepies live here," Space Cat went on.

"So I came to ask if they had heard from their cousins who were living on my planet."

"And have they?" asked Space Dog.

Space Cat looked uncomfortable.
“Well . . .“ she said. “I don't speak very good Threepie.
There was a little mistake . . . and the Threepies won't let me go.”
She sniffed. “I've been here for AGES . . . I'm a prisoner.“
Space Dog jumped up.

“Why?“ he said.
“SSSSH!” Space Cat put her paw to her mouth. “It's a little embarrassing . . . “

Space Dog looked at her.
“What happened?”

“Well . . . “
Space Cat began to whisper.

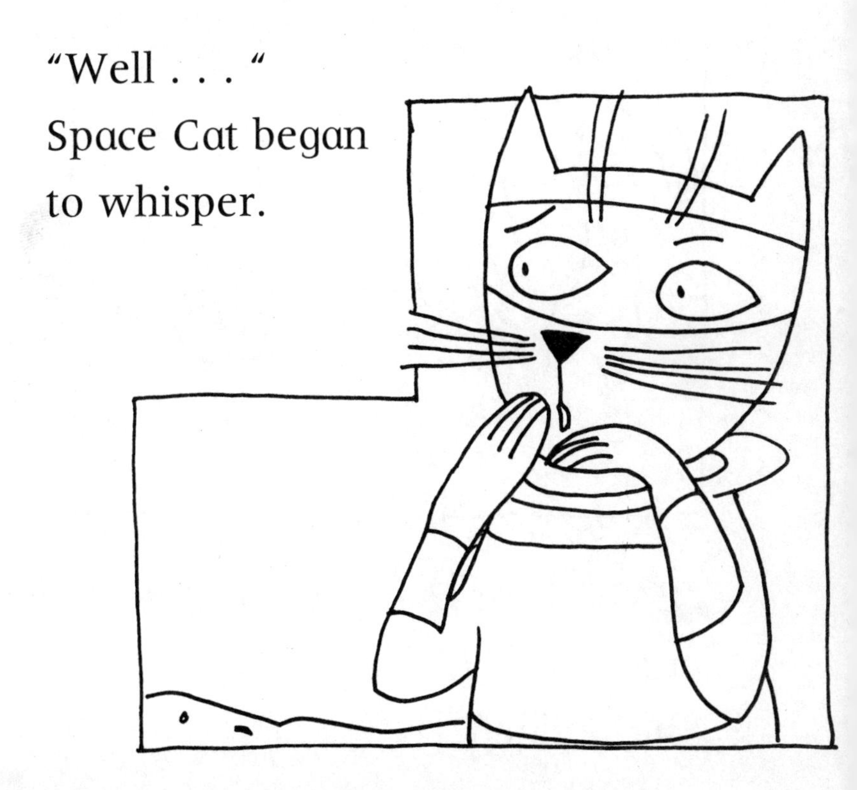

"You see . . . the Threepies think that I've eaten their chief."

"EATEN him?" Space Dog stared at Space Cat.
She nodded.

"Um . . . and was that the mistake?" Space Dog scratched his ear. "You ate him, but didn't mean to?"

"Oh NO!" Space Cat looked shocked. "I'd NEVER do a thing like that." She coughed, and glowed all over. "But I did just . . . pat him."

"Is that all?" said Space Dog.
"Yes." Space Cat's eyes filled with tears and she tweaked at a whisker.

"It's what cats do. They pat things.

But I patted him too hard, and he fell down a black hole. That hole, over there. The other Threepies think I ate him, and now they won't let me go—"

Space Dog covered his ears with his paws.

Space Cat sniffed and wiped her tears on her tail.

"I see," said Space Dog. "Well, there's only one thing to do. We'll have to go down the black hole and get him back."

Chapter Four

Space Dog jumped.
"What is it?"

Space Cat's fur was standing up on end. "WATER! she hissed. "The bottom of the black hole is full of water! I HATE water!!!"

"What a pity," said Space Dog.
"I thought it would be really
useful if you came too . . .
I mean, cats can see in the
dark, can't they?
And it'll be REALLY dark in
that black hole."

Space Cat smoothed down her fur. "You're quite right – I can see in the dark. But if I'm ANYWHERE near water I shut my eyes. So I wouldn't be any help at all."

Space Dog stood up straight.
"I'll do it alone. After all – I
AM Space Dog."

He walked slowly over to the
black hole. It looked very black
indeed.
And very deep.

Space Dog took a deep breath, double flipped over the edge . . .

and
began
slowly

hovering.

It WAS dark. It was so dark that Space Dog felt as though he was going into a huge nothingness.

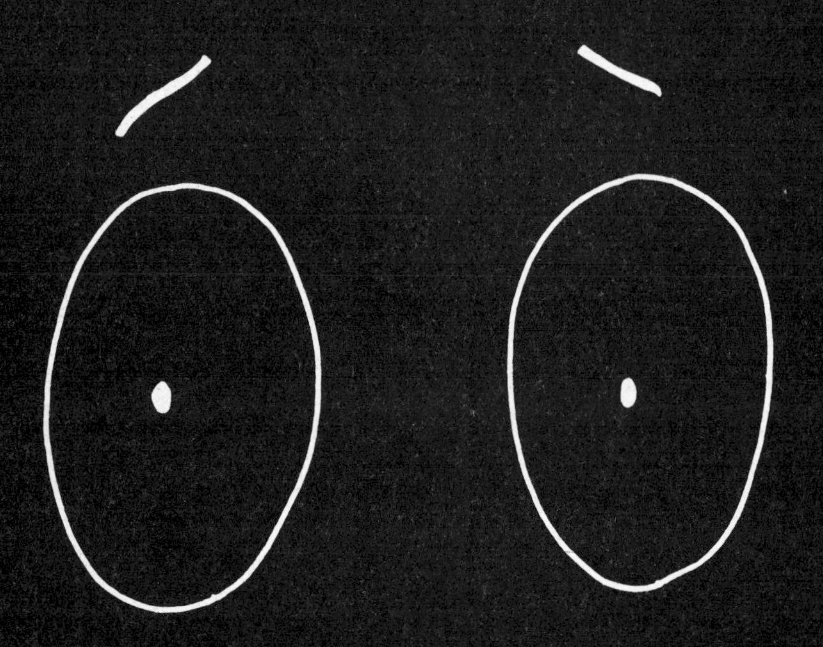

This is dreadful," he said to himself. "How will I ever find anything in here?" But he went on down . . . and down . . . and down.
"WHAT WAS THAT?"

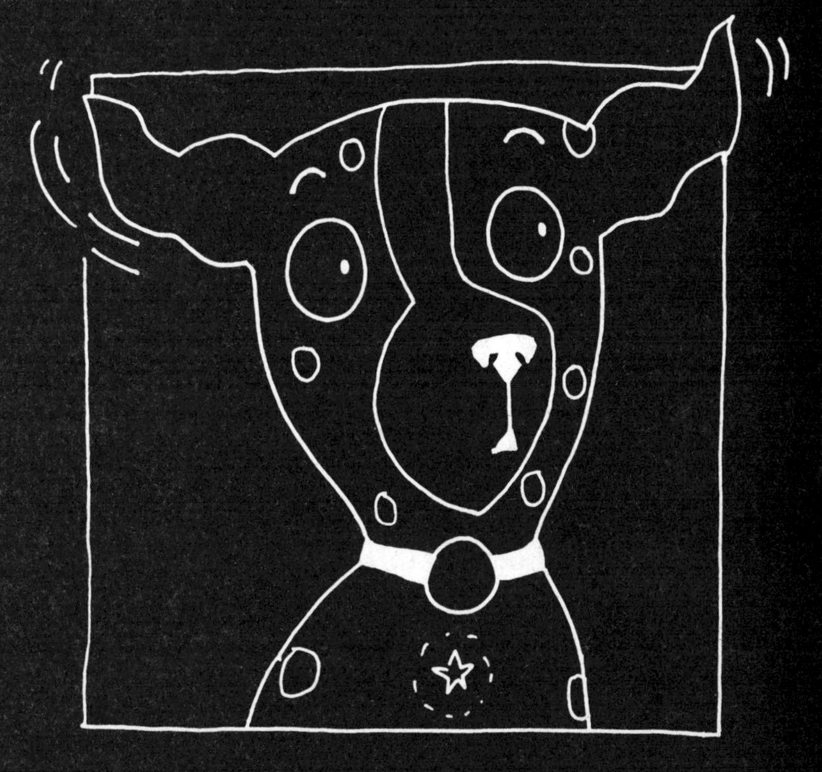

Space Dog twitched his ears into Super Listen Mode.

Yes! There was a buzzing. It was very very faint, but he could hear it.

And every now and then there was a little splash.
"Chief!" Space Dog called.
"Chief Threepie?"
The buzzing grew louder.

Space Dog heaved a loud sigh of relief . . . and suddenly there was light. BRIGHT light. SUNLIGHT!

Space Dog could see! And just below him was Chief Threepie, paddling in the water at the bottom of the hole.

"WUZZ! " said the chief.

"AHA!" said Space Dog. He scooped up the chief . Then with one long ZOOOOOOMMMMM!! he flew up to the light.

There was Space Cat, rubbing her eyes in the bright sunshine.

The Threepies were hopping up and down "BUZZZ, WUZZZ!".

Space Dog landed with a neat twist, and put Chief Threepie down, very carefully, on a pebble.

Then he looked up.
"Hello, Big Sun!" he said.
"That was good timing!"

Big Sun beamed. "I came to thank you for catching Little Sun."

Space Dog turned to the Threepies. "Everything is all right now," he said. "Your chief is saved."

"Buzzz wuzzz, Hurrah!"
cheered the Threepies.
"Buzzz CAT wuzzz!"
"They say you're free to go,"
Space Dog told Space Cat.

Space Cat began to purr.
"Could you ask them about my planet?" she said. "PLEASE!"
Space Dog turned back to the buzzing Threepies.

“Zzzzzz Purrgo?” he asked.
The Threepies began to buzz madly. “Buzz BUZZZZ!” they said. “WUZZ!”
Space Dog smiled at Space Cat. “Good news! Purrgo slid down a comet trail . . . you’ll find it in South Outer Space. As good as new!”

"PURRRRR!!" Space cat purred so loudly that Space Dog took a step back.

"Well," he said, "It must be time to go." Then he stopped.

"Er . . . Space Cat. Before you go home . . . would you like to have a cup of tea with me?"

"Lovely," purred Space Cat, and she put her paw in Space Dog's.

"Here you go," Big Sun shouted cheerfully.
He sent down a sunbeam.
And off . . .

and away . . .

they flew . . .